Library of Congress Cataloging in Publication Data:

Matthews, Maria. My little pony, Baby Firefly's adventure and other my little pony stories. SUMMARY: Three stories include "Sundance and the Golden Surprise," "Baby Firefly's Adventure," and "Cuddles Goes to a Party." 1. Children's stories, American. [1. Ponies—Fiction. 2. Short stories] I. Beylon, Catherine M., ill. PZ7.M4342My 1985 [E] 85-42537 ISBN: 0-394-87386-6

Manufactured in the United States of America 3 4 5 6 7 8 9 0

My Little Pony®

Baby Firefly's Adventure
and Other My Little Pony Stories

By Maria Matthews
Illustrated by Cathy Beylon

Random House 🏠 New York

Sundance and the Golden Surprise

It was a bright, sunny morning outside the Lullabye Nursery. The Baby Ponies were galloping through the meadow playing tag when they noticed their friend Megan sitting beneath a shady oak tree. She looked very unhappy.

"What's wrong, Megan?" asked Baby Blossom.

"Today is Sundance's birthday," said Megan, "and I don't have anything to give her except these ribbons for her halter."

"Those ribbons are a wonderful present," said Baby Blossom.

"And they'll look beautiful on Sundance's halter," said Baby Glory.

"They would have," said Megan sadly. "But Sundance's halter is lost. And I can't look for it because I have to go to school."

"We'll help you find it," said Baby Blossom.

"That's right!" said Baby Glory. "And we'll have a birthday party, too. Bring Sundance here after school. We'll take care of everything else!"

"Thanks, ponies!" said Megan, and she left for school.

"Let's try the Waterfall first," said Baby Blossom, and the two ponies hurried off.

"Hi, ponies!" quacked a voice from under the
Waterfall. The Baby Ponies peered through the foam and
bubbles to see Duck Soup splashing happily in the water.

"Hi, Duck Soup!" said Baby Blossom. "We're helping
Megan find Sundance's halter. Have you seen it?"

"Sundance stopped by for a swim yesterday," quacked
the little duck. "She was wearing the halter then."

"It might still be here!" cried the Baby Ponies eagerly,
and they began to search.

"I'll help too!" said Duck Soup as she climbed out of
the water and joined her friends.

The Baby Ponies searched all around the Waterfall, but they couldn't find Sundance's halter anywhere.

"Maybe we should give up," said Baby Glory.

"Wait—I have an idea!" Duck Soup quacked loudly. Flapping her wings, she waddled back to the Waterfall and plunged into the water. In a moment she reappeared, and in her tiny beak was Sundance's missing halter! "She probably lost it while she was swimming," quacked the little duck.

"But now it's covered with mud!" gasped Baby Blossom.

"We'll have to clean it before Megan and Sundance come over," said Baby Glory. "Let's hurry!"

The Baby Ponies thanked Duck Soup and rushed back to the Lullabye Nursery.

Back at the nursery the Baby Ponies got ready for Sundance's birthday party while Baby Blossom and Baby Glory cleaned the halter. They bustled about happily, making apple cakes and setting the table. Then they hung birthday balloons and put fresh flowers on the table. Finally everything was ready—everything except Sundance's halter!

"I've cleaned and cleaned it," said Baby Blossom with a sigh, "but it doesn't look any better."

"Sparkler will know what to do!" said Baby Surprise. "I'll go get her." And she rushed over to the Dream Castle to get the Little Pony.

Soon Baby Surprise returned with Sparkler, and Baby Glory showed her Sundance's muddy halter.

"Can you make it shine like new?" she asked.

"We can make it better than new!" said Sparkler with a smile. "All it needs is a little sparkle dust!" Then she reached into the small velvet pouch that hung from her neck, and blew a cloud of glittering dust over the halter.

"Now give the sparkle dust time to work. Put the halter in a box, and wrap the box nicely," Sparkler told the babies. "And hurry, because our friends are here!"

The Baby Ponies looked through the window. There was Sundance walking up the path with Megan!

PIN THE TAIL

"Happy birthday, Sundance!" cried the Baby Ponies.
Sundance pranced and nickered with excitement.

Soon everyone was having a wonderful time. They
sang songs, bobbed for apples, and played musical chairs.
"This is the best party ever!" Megan said happily to her
friends.

"Now it's time for Sundance to open her presents!" said
Baby Glory. She laid a beautifully wrapped box in front of
her friend.

"What if Sparkler's dust didn't do anything?" whispered
Baby Blossom to Baby Glory as they waited. "What if the
halter still looks the same?"

"We'll know soon!" said Baby Glory.

Megan gasped as Sundance opened the box. The pony's halter was glittering and sparkling. It was gold! Sundance whinnied with delight. "It's so beautiful! How did you...?"

Sparkler stepped forward and said,

"It doesn't matter if it's old or new
Or whether it's pink, or white, or blue.
But give it in love and then you'll see,
It will become what you want it to be!"

"I almost forgot, Sundance... I have something for you too!" cried Megan. Then she tied her pretty ribbons on either side of the gleaming halter. "Happy birthday!" she cried, and gave Sundance a big hug. "Now you've got the best halter in Pony Land!"

13

Baby Firefly's Adventure

It was dark in the Lullabye Nursery. All the Baby Ponies were sound asleep in their beds—all except Baby Firefly!

"I don't know why I have to go to sleep," she complained with a little snort. "I'm not even tired." She got out of her bed and tiptoed over to where Baby Moondancer lay sleeping. "Pssst! Moondancer, wake up!" whispered Baby Firefly.

Baby Moondancer rubbed her eyes sleepily. "Why aren't you in bed, Firefly?" she mumbled.

"I want to go outside," said Baby Firefly. "I've never stayed up all night. I want to see what happens when everyone is asleep."

"But it's too dark, and we're supposed to be in bed," said Baby Moondancer.

"It will be fun," said Baby Firefly. "And you could light the way!"

Finally Baby Moondancer agreed, and the two ponies crept quietly out the front door of the nursery.

Outside the sky was dark and misty. Baby Firefly and Baby Moondancer sniffed the night air and looked up at the pale thin moon, half hidden by clouds.

"Look over there—real fireflies!" cried Baby Firefly excitedly. The tiny fireflies glittered all around them, lighting up and disappearing before Baby Firefly could catch one.

"Let's go to the pond," said Baby Firefly. "Can you light the way?"

"I think so!" said Baby Moondancer. She tried to remember the special magic she'd learned from her mother. Sure enough, first a faint ray of light appeared from the tip of her unicorn horn and then her whole body began to glow!

"Thanks, Moondancer!" said Baby Firefly. The two ponies set off toward the pond.

Before long they came to a small clearing.

"Which way do we go now?" asked Baby Firefly.

"I'm not sure," said Baby Moondancer. "I'll light up a cloud, and we'll be able to see."

Baby Moondancer pointed her unicorn horn at a large puffy cloud above, stomped her little hoofs twice, and sent a spray of sparks shooting into the air. Suddenly the cloud lit up in beautiful shades of pink, yellow, and ivory.

"Gosh—it looks like a firecracker!" gasped Baby Firefly as she flew above the treetops and looked around. "There's the pond—it's just ahead!" Baby Firefly landed next to her friend and they hurried off.

At the pond a bullfrog croaked from a nearby lily pad, and tree toads warbled in the bushes. Suddenly the ponies heard a quack and a rustling in the reeds, and Duck Soup came paddling into the middle of the pond. "Is it morning?" she asked sleepily.

"No," said Baby Firefly with a laugh. "Baby Moondancer lit up a cloud so that we could find our way in the dark."

"We wanted to see what night was like," added Moondancer.

By the light of the shining cloud, the Baby Ponies splashed and played in the pond with Duck Soup. They swam races, chased fireflies, and skipped stones.

"This is much more fun than being in bed!" said Baby Firefly happily. "I'll never go to sleep again!"

They were still splashing in the pond when they heard a loud CRASH! Suddenly lightning streaked across the sky and the cloud became dark.

"What happened to your cloud?" cried Baby Firefly.

"I don't know," said Baby Moondancer. The Baby Ponies were very frightened.

"Let's hurry home," said Baby Firefly.

"I hope we can find the way!" cried Baby Moondancer. The sky was very dark.

Just then it lit up again. BOOM! CRASH! The thunder seemed to be coming closer!

"Baby Moondancer—where are you?" cried Baby Firefly. "I can't see!" she whimpered. "I'm scared!"

Baby Firefly blinked her eyes and looked around. She was in her bed, warm and dry, and Baby Moondancer was sound asleep in her little bed nearby. "It was all a dream!" said Baby Firefly.

But outside there *was* a great thunderstorm! Baby Firefly watched the rain pour off the roof of the Lullabye Nursery and the lightning bolts race across the sky. Soon she became very sleepy. "Sometimes dreaming is more exciting than being awake!" she thought happily. "I'll never mind going to sleep again!"

After all, she had been out in a thunderstorm, and had never even gotten wet!

19

Cuddles Goes to a Party

It was a sunny day in Pony Land. Inside the Lullabye
Nursery the Baby Ponies were playing with their dolls.
Some had been put to bed, others sat on chairs, and the
rest were having their clothes changed.

"I'm tired of dolls! They're boring!" said Baby Surprise,
throwing her favorite dolly down. "I want a real baby to
play with!" She ran down the nursery stairs and out the
front door.

Out in the yard, Lickety-Split was sitting under a tree eating an ice cream cone. The Baby Buggy was parked nearby.

"What's inside the buggy?" asked Baby Surprise as she admired the buggy's lacy pink cover, its lavender and lace parasol, and its lavender wheels.

"A baby," said Lickety-Split. "Her name is Cuddles. She's sound asleep."

Baby Surprise peeked into the buggy. There was the prettiest baby she'd ever seen, wearing a little lace cap tied with a pink ribbon. As Baby Surprise watched, Cuddles woke up and smiled at her.

"Please, Lickety-Split, may I play with Cuddles?" asked
Baby Surprise.

"Well, all right," said Lickety-Split. "You may take her
for a walk. But be very careful. Remember, she's only a
little baby."

"I will," promised Baby Surprise. The baby cooed and
gurgled while they walked, and she laughed when a
butterfly landed on the tip of her nose.

"You're much more fun than a silly old doll," said
Baby Surprise happily.

Suddenly Cuddles stopped gurgling and cooing. She began to squirm. Then she kicked off her blankets. And then she began to cry!

"Hush, hush," said Baby Surprise. "We'll keep walking and you'll feel better." But the faster they walked, the louder Cuddles yelled. She yelled so hard that her face turned pinker than the ribbon on her cap!

Baby Surprise began to get very worried. Why
wouldn't Cuddles stop crying? Just then Baby Surprise
noticed the Baby Ponies sitting under a tree. They were
having a tea party with their favorite dolls.

"Let's go to the tea party, Cuddles," said Baby Surprise.
"Maybe that will cheer you up." She took Cuddles' blanket
and laid it on the grass. Then she put the baby down. "You
can be my doll and have something to eat," said Baby
Surprise. "Won't that be nice?"

"WAAAAAH!!" wailed Cuddles loudly.

The Baby Ponies had all kinds of treats for their dolls—
sliced apples, carrots, and little oat cakes. "Here, Cuddles.
You have some too," said Baby Blossom, and she gave
Cuddles a tiny slice of apple. But Cuddles wouldn't open
her mouth. She scrunched up her face, pushed the apple
away, and let out a howl.

"You'll make a mess of your pretty blanket," said Baby
Surprise. "Now try some tea."

"WAAAAAH!!" Cuddles screamed loudly, and the tea
spilled all over her dress.

"What's wrong?" asked Baby Cotton Candy.

"Why won't she stop crying?" asked Baby Moondancer.

"Can we do anything to help?" asked Baby Blossom.

"I don't know!" cried Baby Surprise, who was almost in tears herself.

Just then Cuddles began to crawl away. Before Baby Surprise could catch her, Cuddles spilled the rest of the tea and tipped over all the little plates. "She's making such a mess!" wailed Baby Surprise. The other ponies just looked at their well-behaved dolls.

"I think Cuddles is ready for another bottle," said Lickety-Split, coming toward them. She wiped Cuddles' face and put her back in the Baby Buggy. "Thank you for taking such good care of her," she said, and she pushed the buggy away.

Baby Surprise sighed with relief.

"Have some tea," said Baby Blossom.

"And some cake. It will make you feel better," said Baby Moondancer.

"That would be wonderful," said Baby Surprise. "But first there's something I have to do." And she ran back to the nursery as fast as she could.

There was her favorite doll, lying in a heap on the floor. "I'm so glad to see you!" cried Baby Surprise, giving it a great big hug. "You're not boring at all. You're the best dolly a Baby Pony could have!"

Then Baby Surprise and her doll went back to the tea party and had a very good time together indeed.

Splasher

Who's making all the waves wash high?
Who's causing the commotion?
It's Splasher churning up the foam.
She's stirring up the ocean!

Sea Star

Star light, star bright—
Sea Star floats by day and night.
Her little head is full of wishes
She hears from all the silver fishes.

Sea Shimmer

When sunbeams dance across the sea
And blue waves start to glimmer,
You'll see a pony bobble by—
It's sweet, demure Sea Shimmer.

Backstroke

When you need a teacher, you need one who knows
How to float in the moat—and wiggle her toes.
Ask Backstroke to show you, you'll see it's a breeze,
In the blink of an eye you'll be swimming with ease!

Surfrider

Surfrider is daring and skillful and brave
As she skims along on the top of each wave.
No one can catch her, for she's very fast,
Never, but never, will *she* come in last!

Tiny Bubbles

When the ponies need seafoam and bubbles
To keep their manes shiny and clean,
Tiny Bubbles will blow you some doubles,
The biggest that you've ever seen!